T0363147

DINOSAURS AND DRAGONS

ROSE SIVA

Published by Boolarong Press,
655 Toohey Road
Salisbury Qld 4107
Australia.
www.boolarongpress.com.au

 A catalogue record for this
book is available from the
National Library of Australia

ISBN: 9781925522617

Printed and bound by Watson Ferguson & Company, Salisbury, Australia

CONTENTS

Thanks to all the wonderful, dedicated people who have found, dug up and prepped dinosaur bones in far west Queensland. You have all inspired my dinosaur journey. And special thanks to Lyn and Wendy for their patient persistent proof reading and editing skills.

CHAPTER 1

As far as Josh could remember, it had all started on Grandpa's birthday. His Mum had organised lunch for the rellies – she was big on organising family gatherings. She believed family was really important, and since Grandma's death she made sure Grandpa was included in all family gatherings, no matter how big or small. And this was his birthday so she had arranged for all the family to be there. It didn't matter that Grandpa didn't want the fuss.

After lunch all the adults sat around the table talking and the kids were shooed out into the yard to play. Suddenly five year old Emily burst into the room with Josh close behind. Almost in tears, her face red and puffy, her chest was heaving as she gasped for breath.

"It's not true," she sobbed. "What Josh just said – it's not true! He's telling fibs!"

Emily's mum Pam immediately opened her arms, pulled her close and hugged her, trying to quiet the child. "Now, now, pet, it's OK, just take some deep breaths," she soothed. "There, there, now tell mummy what's the problem."

Emily turned her tear-streaked face to her mother. "Josh said unicorns and dragons and dinosaurs didn't exist!" she blurted. "But they did! There are pictures of them in my books!"

Josh stood defiantly at the door. At ten, he was old enough to know some things were made up. He'd just finished a unit at school on fact or fiction.

"They're just made up," he declared. "Just pictures someone has dreamed up."

Distraught, Emily looked up at her mother's face, seeking reassurance. There was a few minutes silence that, to Emily seemed to go on forever.

The adults looked at each other across the table.

"Well," said Grandpa, "there are some mythical creatures we like to believe did exist, but I can assure you dinosaurs definitely did exist, even in Australia."

Josh looked across at Grandpa. "But Jurassic Park – it was all made up, Grandpa. It was a movie with models and computer generated images. I saw on TV how they made it all up."

"That may be so, Josh," continued Grandpa, "but it was based on real fossil bones of real dinosaurs. We may not be exactly sure what they looked like, but from the fossils that have been found we have a pretty good idea."

"But anyway, that was in America or an island in Hawaii or somewhere. Not in Australia," continued

Josh defiantly. He wasn't prepared to lose this argument. He was going to stand his ground.

"You're wrong there, my boy," said Grandpa. "I've seen real dinosaur bones right here in Australia. Right here in Queensland, actually."

There was another silence as Josh absorbed this information. Dinosaurs in Australia? Really? He knew better than to argue further, especially with Grandpa, who as far as he knew had never told a fib. Even about the tooth fairy. When Mum had told him to leave his tooth under his pillow and he had lost it instead, Grandpa had said, 'That's OK – the tooth fairy is something Mum and Dad made up so you wouldn't feel sad when you lost a tooth. The tooth fairy is pretend, so she won't be upset you lost your tooth.'

Josh turned and went outside. Emily stopped snivelling and looked much happier. Grandpa had said dinosaurs, and therefore unicorns and dragons did exist. Her world was OK again.

And the grown-ups started talking about other things.

CHAPTER 2

It was several months later, a couple of weeks before the school holidays, when Josh found out what was going to happen. It seemed Grandpa had taken the dinosaur conversation to heart and had decided it was time his grandchildren found out about dinosaurs in Australia. Grandpa's plan was to take them out to far west Queensland. He owned a camper – he and Grandma had used it on their gem fossicking trips when she was still alive. She had died four years ago and Grandpa hadn't been out west since. He'd lost interest, Josh guessed. He figured life wasn't the same without Grandma.

Anyway, the adults had finally agreed with Grandpa's plan. It would work, but only if Auntie Pam went as well to keep an eye on Grandpa and to manage the kids. So, this school holidays, for three weeks, Grandpa was going to take them out and show them where the dinosaurs had lived. Australian dinosaurs.

Josh's mum was reluctant to burden Grandpa with Josh. She was a school teacher, so usually had time off during the school holidays, and could look after him. But these holidays she had to do something called in-service training. She would normally have arranged for him to stay with his father, but his Dad's fly-in fly-out roster at the mines was not going to work for these holidays. Anyway, she said, his Dad was such a kid himself and so irresponsible, she felt when Josh stayed with him it was like two kids living together, and would only result in both of them getting into trouble.

Since his parents had started living apart his mum seemed happier. There were a lot less arguments, and as Josh had got older he felt more responsible, more like the man of the house, and his Mum treated him much more like an adult.

The only other alternative was for Josh to go into school holiday care. Not only was it expensive – something his mother couldn't really afford – but Josh hated the thought. He would be eleven this year, and he resented the thought of going to a 'child minding' service. So Mum had been persuaded to go along with Grandpa's plan. Auntie Pam worked part time and could take the time off. It did mean Emily would have to come too though ...

But there was another surprise. Cousin Kat, Mum's brother's daughter, was going to come too. Kat, aged fifteen, was older than her cousin Josh. Josh had met her and her Dad, Peter, a few times at family Christmas celebrations and at Grandma's funeral. They lived somewhere way out in the country, so Kat had to go to boarding school in Sydney. Josh had no idea what had happened to her mother – nobody talked about that and he didn't like to ask. Kat was cool; she was sensible, more like a grown up. She read a lot and was interesting to talk to. Not like the catty, whiny, gossipy girls in his class. She was more like a cross between a tomboy and a grownup.

Kat was going to fly in from Sydney instead of going to her Dad's place for the school holidays, and she was going to travel with them. Grandpa would have all his grandkids with him – Josh, Emily and Kat. A Grandpa's Road Trip, with Auntie Pam to make sure everything was OK.

CHAPTER 3

Grandpa was getting his camper ready. He said it wasn't really a 'camper' – it was a 'slide-on' bolted on the tray of his ute, with steps at the back. Inside was a little fridge, a really small kitchen bench and a cooker. A small double bed sat over the cab of the ute, and the seat opposite the kitchen bench could be used as another bed. Not much room. Not much room at all for two adults and three kids.

The plan was for Auntie Pam and Emily to sleep on the double bed over the cab and Grandpa to sleep in the other bed inside. The older children would sleep outside – Josh in a tent and Kat had a swag. A swag – how cool was that! Josh wished he had a swag to sleep in instead of having to sleep in a tent. He had looked them up on the internet – a swag was a rolled up sleeping bag and mattress all in one that you rolled out on the ground. He was intrigued about how come Kat had one – it wasn't the sort of thing he thought teenage girls would like. Not that he knew much about teenage girls apart from programs on TV and the girls in his class. He was keen to find out more about Kat.

Grandpa said they could live on sausages. He had a BBQ that would work off the gas bottle on the rack on the back of the camper. But Auntie Pam and Mum had other ideas, and it seemed Auntie Pam was going to organise the food. No doubt it would be 'healthy' and involve vegetables. But Josh knew Grandpa loved tomato sauce and hopefully there would be lots of that he could use to disguise the taste. Josh had 'camped out' in Grandpa's back yard and Grandpa had lit a fire, so he had an idea of what camping might be like. He was quite looking forward to it.

+++

Mum had come into his bedroom one evening as he was getting ready for bed. "Joshua," she started, and Josh immediately tensed. No conversation with Mum that started with 'Joshua' worked out well. He sat on his bed and she sat next to him.

"Joshua, I need you to do something for me on this trip. You know Grandpa has great ideas for the trip and he's looking forward so much to taking you to some really outback places. But Grandpa isn't as young as he used to be – you know he'll be seventy five this year?"

Josh didn't – he hadn't really thought about Grandpa's age.

"He hasn't been camping since Grandma died," continued his mother. "And she used to take care of Grandpa and make sure everything went smoothly. Auntie Pam will be there to take care of you too, but she hasn't been camping in years, and as far as I know she's never been to the outback. It's very different to Brisbane and the Gold Coast."

She sat silently for a while. Josh didn't quite know where this conversation was going.

"I know you're only ten, almost eleven, but you're the next oldest male on the trip. I need you to keep an eye on Grandpa for me – for all of us. You're a very sensible boy – young man – much more sensible than your father. Thank goodness for that!"

She smiled and Josh started to relax. He knew what Mum meant. Dad could be a bit irresponsible – Mum called him a 'loose cannon' sometimes.

"I don't mean take over, but just use your common sense to make sure the trip goes smoothly. Make sure Grandpa checks the oil and fuel in the truck every day, and checks the maps and the road conditions. And whatever you do, don't let him drive at night. I've heard how dangerous some of those outback roads can be, and how many vehicles hit kangaroos at dawn and dusk. Be his right hand man. Will you promise me you'll do that?"

Josh leaned against his mother. "Of course I will Mum," he said. "Grandpa and I get along really well. I'll make sure everything runs like a well-oiled clock."

They both grinned. That was one of Grandpa's favourite sayings.

Later, curled up in his warm bed, Josh felt both older and taller. His Mum trusted him to be a responsible adult on the trip and it made him feel, well, different. Much more grown up and valued – part of the team.

He was really looking forward to this trip.

CHAPTER 4

Kat flew into the Gold Coast airport the day before they were due to leave on their road trip. She had excess baggage – her swag was too big to go as general luggage, so it went to the oversize baggage area. Josh went with her to pick it up, swung it across his back and carried it to the car. They headed back to Josh's house for the final night before their trip.

The camper was packed and seats were sorted out in the ute. Auntie Pam, Emily and Grandpa were to travel in the front, and Josh and Kat were to be in the back seat. Auntie Pam had made a comment that if Josh and Kat were going to fight in the back she would make one of them swap with Emily. Not likely, they both agreed. Neither wanted to sit next to Emily or Auntie Pam!

Grandpa greeted Kat warmly. She was almost as tall as him and looked really fit and healthy. Glowing almost.

"Farm life suits you," he said. "You look like a lady of the land."

"Thanks Grandpa," she replied. "Yes, I love it on the land and can't wait for the school holidays so I can go home. There are a few other kids at the boarding school who also come from cattle stations, so I do have friends who think the same way I do."

Josh was curious about Kat. Her life seemed to be very different to his on the Gold Coast.

Grandpa spread a map of Queensland out on the table. He had circled some place names. Gold Coast. Mount Morgan. Rubyvale. Richmond. Winton.

"We're heading inland to an area that used to be a great inland sea millions of years ago. That's where the dinosaurs lived."

"Isn't that pretty much where the Great Artesian Basin is?" asked Kat.

"Sure is, young Kat. You know your Australian geography, young lady. It's pretty dry and dusty now – you wouldn't recognise it as a sea," he continued. "Your Grandma and I used to go out there looking for gems and opals and the like." He looked reflective and a little sad as he continued. "We found all sorts of things, including fossils."

"Did you find any unicorns?" Emily piped up.

"Well, not that we recognised, but then I'm no expert on unicorns," he said, evading the question. Josh caught his Mum's warning eye and got the look – *Don't butt in, boy – leave that subject alone!*

"So, we have a bit of a drive ahead of us. It'll take us quite a few days to get out there, so I want to leave early in the morning. You need to be ready by seven o'clock."

"You need to bring something to do in the ute – a book or a game or something to do to pass the time," said Auntie Pam, already practising being 'in control' of the kids.

"We can bring our iPads, and phones," interjected Josh.

"Don't depend too much on those things, boy," Grandpa replied. "There's not much mobile coverage where we're heading, and I don't have any power points to recharge gadgets in the camper. We'll be depending on the solar panels to give us enough power to use the lights at night, and we're going to cook on camp fires or the gas cooker. The only place you can recharge your gadgets will be the auxiliary plug in the ute. And there's only one and you can only use that when the ute is running. Last thing we want is a flat battery. Anyway, do you kids good to live without your gadgets for a while. They give you square eyes."

That was another one of Grandpa's favourite sayings whenever he saw them on their iPads or phones. But was he serious about no mobile coverage? Surely not, thought Josh. There was coverage everywhere, wasn't there? How could people keep in touch without mobiles?

CHAPTER 5

True to his word, Grandpa parked his camper in Josh's Mum's driveway at 6:30am. Auntie Pam and Emily were already there, and she was in full control mode.

"Joshua, Katherine – get your bags out there on the driveway for Grandpa to load. And remember, he said only one bag each. Joshua, you help Grandpa lift the bags up into the camper. Katherine, you make sure you both have what you need in the cab of the ute."

Josh silently wondered how this was going to work. He and Kat had already started calling her

Sergeant Major Pam behind her back. And he knew Grandpa didn't like being ordered around. Mum had enough trouble when she tried, in the nicest possible way, to organise him. "Leave me alone, woman. I'm a big boy and I didn't come down in the last shower," was his usual response.

"Mount Morgan tonight," he stated. "It's only 650ks and we could go further, but your Auntie Pam says that's far enough for one day. Me and Grandma used to go all the way to Emerald in one day, so I don't know what all the fuss is about," he grumbled. "Seems you kids are all a bit delicate. Maybe you need to toughen up a bit."

Mum attempted to soothe the waters. "Come on, Grandpa," she said. "You're not as young as you used to be, and you know how I feel about you driving in the dark. That's more than enough kilometres and plenty far enough in one day."

Grandpa made the harrumphing noise he liked to make when he didn't agree, but wasn't going to argue. Josh passed the bags up, and he put them on the floor of the camper. Josh was going to have to keep an eye on Grandpa if he was going to keep his promise to his Mum.

CHAPTER 6

"How are we off for fuel?" Josh asked when they pulled in at Gympie for a break.

"Used three quarters of a tank." replied Grandpa. "I have two fuel tanks, but you're right, it would be a good idea to fuel up here. Fuel's going to get more expensive as we head west. Thanks for the reminder, Josh."

Josh felt quite grown up, and definitely part of the team. But he did bristle when Auntie Pam reminded him and Kat to go to the toilet before they got back in the ute. Kat looked down and he was sure he could see her smirking. "Yes, Sergeant Major Pam," she muttered quietly.

They made it to Mount Morgan by late afternoon. Grandpa's ute was quite noisy, so there wasn't much conversation between the front and the back seats. Grandpa drove slower than Josh's father did, but he did have a camper unit on the back and Auntie Pam sitting next to him. She had made several suggestions about stopping to rest, but apart from a lunch break at the fuel stop, Grandpa kept driving. Josh and Kat had a road map in the back and were able to track their progress. Mount Morgan turned out to be a really small town, but it had a camping ground

"Grandma and I used to free camp at Dululu," Grandpa grumbled as Auntie Pam pointed to the signs.

"You have the children with you, remember, and there are no facilities, no showers or toilets when you're free camping. We need to stay at a proper camping ground," insisted Auntie Pam.

So Grandpa reluctantly checked into the camping ground. He parked in a shady spot under a tree not far from the amenities building. Auntie Pam took Emily to the toilet and Josh and Kat went exploring, while Grandpa set up camp.

"So what's with Mount Morgan?" asked Josh, starting the conversation. "Can't see any mountain around here," he added. It was a bit hilly, but no big mountains with snow or anything.

"It's a mountain range," replied Kat. "I think there used to be a mine here – a gold mine, I think. But they don't mine anymore." Josh had noticed the old buildings as they drove through the town. Some had dates on them, from the late 1800s. The town looked as if it had been around for a long time.

When they walked back to the camper, Grandpa had put down the steps at the back and had pulled out Josh's tent and Kat's swag. It sounded as if he and Auntie Pam were arguing.

"You can't expect her to sleep in that!" Auntie Pam snapped. "It's not safe and it's not suitable for a young girl to sleep in the open."

"Humbug!" retorted Grandpa. "Course she can – that's what she does when she's out on the cattle station with her father. Best thing, sleeping out under the stars."

"It's not safe," retorted Auntie Pam. "She should be inside the tent with Josh."

"Well, we'll let her decide, shall we?" responded Grandpa, obviously not wanting to start an argument with Auntie Pam – not this early in the trip.

In the end it was resolved. Yes, Kat did prefer to sleep under the stars rather than share the tent with Josh, but Auntie Pam insisted she put her swag between the camper and Josh's tent, close in so she would be safe.

Safe from what, wondered Josh.

CHAPTER 7

For dinner, Grandpa cooked sausages and onions on a BBQ plate in the camping ground fire pit, and Auntie Pam cooked some green vegetables as well. Afterwards, they sat on the camp chairs watching the flickering flames. The light cast eerie shadows on their faces and Emily cuddled into Auntie Pam's lap, her eyes drooping in a sleepy daze.

"So why is this place called Mount Morgan?" asked Josh. "Doesn't seem to be much of a mountain."

"Well, I believe it was named after the miner who found gold here," explained Grandpa. "There's a mine where they found gold, silver and copper. It was once the largest gold mine in the world. There used to be a mountain, but they mined it and there's pretty much only a huge hole now. It doesn't operate any more – it's all closed up."

"So it's sort of a ghost town?" asked Josh, wondering if that was what Auntie Pam meant by 'keeping Kat safe'.

Grandpa laughed. "No doubt there might be the ghosts of some miners around – it used to be a pretty rough game back then. Health and safety wasn't a big thing in the olden days. Folks just got on with their lives and were responsible for themselves, before the 'nanny state' we have now with all this occupational health and safety stuff." This was one of Grandpa's hobby horses. He had very strong opinions on people being left alone to learn from their own mistakes, and kids not being 'molly coddled', as he put it. Josh and his mother had talked about this, about Grandpa's views on what children should or shouldn't be allowed to do. His mother said he was right up to a point, but kids still had to have boundaries and not do stuff that was dangerous, especially where they could get hurt or cause damage, like playing with fire and riding a bike without a helmet. Auntie Pam, on the other hand, had a different view. Children should be supervised all the time and not take any risks. This was going to be an interesting trip, and Josh thought it wouldn't be long before there would be more arguments. He'd put money on Grandpa winning. Maybe Auntie Pam would get in a huff, take Emily, and go home and leave Grandpa to it. That would be good – just Grandpa and Kat and himself. They could have some really good adventures ... Josh was staring into the flickering fire light, imagining what might happen, when Grandpa spoke again.

"There could be some really big ghosts here, though. If I remember right, they found some dinosaur footprints here, and the weird thing is, they were on the roof of a cave. Imagine that –

dinosaurs dancing on the ceiling. Must have been quite a dinosaur party," he smiled.

Josh snapped back to the conversation, leaving his thoughts in the firelight. Dinosaurs? Dinosaur footprints on the ceiling of a cave? Really? Right. This was Grandpa winding up Emily again – trying to get her going about dinosaurs being real. But it didn't work. Emily was already asleep on Auntie Pam's lap.

Auntie Pam shooed them all off to bed, but not without another protest about Kat sleeping in the open. Kat didn't comment. She just let it all roll over her as she got her swag ready and slipped into it. Josh lay awake for a while, listening to the noises outside his tent, thinking about what it might be like to sleep in the open. Did her head get cold, and what if a dingo came through the camp ... or a dinosaur? Silly stuff. There were no dinosaurs any more, probably not ever.

CHAPTER 8

Josh woke to soft noises outside. It took him a while to realise he was not at home in his bed, he was in a tent at Mount Morgan. He clambered out of his sleeping bag and out of his tent to find Grandpa and Kat sitting on camp chairs around the fire pit. Grandpa had the fire going and a billy full of water coming to the boil getting ready to make a cuppa. Grandpa liked a cup of tea first thing in the morning.

"How'd you sleep, boy?" asked Grandpa. "Dream about dinosaurs?" Grandpa always liked to call him 'boy' when his mother was not around. She hated it. 'Call him Josh,' she would say. 'The boy has a name – use it.' And Grandpa seemed determined to wind him up about the whole dinosaur thing.

Kat smiled. Josh was slightly envious of Kat. It was obvious she and Grandpa got on well and had a comfortable relationship. He treated her much like a grown up, whereas Josh was very much still a 'boy'.

"Short day today," said Grandpa. "Only 350ks to Rubyvale, so we should be there around lunchtime. Give us time to go out to the gem fossicking areas. That is, if the others get out of bed."

Right on cue Auntie Pam and Emily emerged from the camper, both wearing dressing gowns and fluffy slippers. Quite a contrast to the three sitting around the fire dressed in jeans and jerseys. They disappeared off to the toilet block to have showers and get dressed, leaving Grandpa to organise breakfast – after he had finished his cuppa.

Grandpa had it all sorted and knew where everything was. Josh was impressed by how efficient he was. Mostly he had seen Grandpa sitting back watching other people do things. There were always women around who seemed to take over and do all that stuff. But now he set to work. Iron plate onto the BBQ, bacon and eggs from the esky, plates and cutlery from the box marked 'kitchen'. Kat found the bread and deftly held the slices of bread on a wire rack over the hot fire coals to make toast. Josh didn't do anything – they had it all sorted and didn't need any help.

Auntie Pam and Emily returned, showered and hair brushed, to find breakfast cooked and the tea made. Auntie Pam looked a bit surprised. She assumed she would do all that. When she asked if the others had showered, Grandpa harrumphed and muttered something under his breath about how too much washing weakens the body. But then he added, "We'll be in Rubyvale in plenty of time to have one tonight."

The bacon was great, and the eggs were soft inside, just the way Josh liked them. Actually, better than the way Mum cooked them. Or maybe they just tasted better because he was eating outside.

Auntie Pam took the dishes to the camp kitchen to wash up, leaving Kat, Josh and Grandpa to pack up the camp. Kat helped Josh fold up his tent small enough to get it back in the tent bag. It had come out of the bag easy enough, but folding it up the right way to get it back in was another thing altogether. Kat didn't say anything, she just came over after she had put her swag by the camper. She lifted the edges of the tent to straighten them out into a square, indicated to Josh how to fold it in half and then in thirds, and then she rolled it and Josh held the bag while she slid it in. Easy – she had obviously done this many times before. He reflected again on how different her life was compared with his. Living out on a cattle station, he didn't even know where, with only her Dad – that was probably why she was so comfortable with

Grandpa and he with her. Being used to living with an adult male and no mother, she could look after herself.

As they set off for Rubyvale he made up his mind he was going to find out more about Kat.

CHAPTER 9

Grandpa stopped for fuel at Emerald. He said there might not be fuel at Rubyvale, but even if there was it would probably be more expensive. He opened the bonnet of the ute and asked Josh to check the oil. Josh had done that before, back on the Gold Coast at Grandpa's place. It was a 'thing' they did together, something blokes do. Grandpa had shown Josh the various parts of the motor and how to check the oil and water. Josh felt good – this was something he could do and it made him somehow feel responsible and just a bit more capable – like Kat was.

Rubyvale was very different. From the time they turned off the main road towards Sapphire, the scenery changed. The buildings were mostly built of corrugated iron, and there were piles of dirt everywhere, where holes had been dug, presumably by fossickers looking for gems. Some more elaborate buildings had signs outside saying 'Gems for Sale', and 'Gems Cut Here'. Auntie Pam was looking very uncomfortable.

"Is this where you used to bring Grandma?" she asked. "People don't really live out here like this, do they?"

"Sure do," responded Grandpa. "A lot of people are only here during the winter – only a few live here full time. It gets pretty hot out here in the summer. We used to come here most winters for a month or two – we'd camp out in the fossicking area near Rubyvale. These houses in town in Rubyvale are pretty flash compared to the humpies out on the fossicking areas. Most people have an old caravan or a bus or something similar. I guess you wouldn't be very pleased if I took you out there to camp, so we'll set up camp in the camping ground in Rubyvale and then I'll take you sight-seeing."

Auntie Pam looked very unimpressed.

It didn't take long to choose a campsite in the camping ground, under the trees not far from the toilet block. Grandpa and Kat tied a tarp between two trees to make a shady area, and they unloaded the tent, swag, chairs and other gear and set it all out in the shade. Auntie Pam expressed concern about leaving things in the open where, she said, there was nothing to stop things getting stolen, but Grandpa overruled her.

"This is Rubyvale, woman. There are different rules out here. You don't steal other people's stuff, and you don't take anything from someone else's mine either. That's called 'ratting', and ratters find themselves at the bottom of a mine shaft in the dark of night. Probably with broken legs." Grandpa was starting to set his rules – this was his trip.

They spent the afternoon in the fossicking areas. Grandpa showed them where he and Grandma used to camp at an area called Reward. It was rough, very rough. The road out to Reward was badly rutted with big holes, and Grandpa had to put the ute into four wheel drive at one place where they crossed down into a dry river bed and up the bank on the other side. They stopped at one place, where Grandpa talked to someone who was living in an old bus with a corrugated iron shelter built on the side. It looked as if the bus had been there forever, and Josh thought the man looked as if he had been there forever as well. Grandpa asked after some people he and Grandma used to know, but apparently they weren't there anymore.

They travelled very slowly. Grandpa stopped every so often to tell them about the area and where the miners worked. He explained that most of the mining was underground. The miners dug tunnels looking for particular soil patterns, and when they found what they were looking for, they would haul the soil up to the surface and wash it, looking for gemstones. Hot, dry, dirty work. Josh couldn't imagine anyone wanting to do that. But apparently some people had been doing it for years and years. The children and Auntie Pam were all very quiet, listening intently to Grandpa talking, taking in this completely alien-looking world. Finally Grandpa said, "OK, enough for the afternoon. Let's go back to town and have a cuppa. We can stay here another night, and I'll show you some of the gems at the gem dealers tomorrow. Then you can see what they're finding and why they do this. It's very addictive when you get started, and some people come back every year like Grandma and I used to, they get hooked, and stay here all year round."

Auntie Pam's expression said it all – she didn't have to say anything. This was absolutely not a fit place to live, even for a short time. And Josh was inclined to agree with her. No power, no water, no internet, just annoying flies and the heat. He'd give it a miss too, but he kept his opinion to himself.

CHAPTER 10

That evening they lit another camp fire, and after they'd showered at Auntie Pam's insistence, they sat around the fire talking. Grandpa told them about the area, taking in Sapphire, Rubyvale, Anakie and another place called Willow. Places rich in gems that had been formed and 'spat out' of volcanoes 50 million years ago. The gems looked like little pebbles and were mostly sapphires, which apparently came in different colours and shades.

"The trick is in knowing one when you see it. They're not very colourful in their natural state," explained Grandpa. "But when they're cut they can be really beautiful. I found a lovely sapphire that we had cut and made into a ring for your Grandma. It was worth a lot of money, but it was worth even more to us because I found it and gave it to your Grandma."

They sat in silence for a moment.

"Tomorrow I'll take you to a mine that's open to the public, so you can see what it looks like underground. We'll go to a gem cutter too, so you can see how the stones are cut and how beautiful they look."

Josh hadn't ever heard Grandpa talking about things in those terms – about stones being beautiful, and about Grandma. He started to understand how much Grandpa had loved Grandma, and how much he missed her. They had done this together, coming out to the Gemfields looking for gems.

They sat quietly. Then Kat broke the silence. "Did you find any fossils here?" she asked.

"No, not really. Maybe a few, but we weren't searching for fossils. We found more out at Lightning Ridge when we were looking for opals. If I remember rightly, the great inland sea didn't extend to cover the land this far east, and the volcanoes that formed around this area were much younger than the sea – they formed only 50 million years ago. Don't you have to go back to 100 million years or older to get fossils?"

"Yes, I think you're right," said Kat. "I think the last inland sea retreated around 100 million years ago, and the dinosaurs were here after that, living on the forest that grew after the water went away. And if this area wasn't covered by the sea, there wouldn't be marine fossils either."

"I'm pretty sure we need to be further inland to get fossils. Dinosaurs didn't dance around here much, especially on ceilings." Grandpa smiled again.

"Dinosaurs, dinosaurs, dinosaurs and dragons. We're going on a dinosaur and dragon hunt," Emily sang happily.

Yeah, right. Good on you Grandpa, thought Josh. Keep on about dinosaurs dancing on the ceiling.

The mine was not as Josh had imagined it would be. It was quite big and the cavern underground was wide once they got down the narrow passageway. It was well lit and not dark and damp at all. The guide explained how the gemstones were formed, and how they collected in gravel layers in the clay. The miners would follow the gravel layers, digging in the hope of finding gemstones. When Josh mentioned that he thought the mine would be small and dark, Grandpa laughed.

"This mine is just for the tourists," he explained. "Real mines, out in the fossicking areas or on the leases, are dark, narrow, and steep. Most have ladders to get down to the lower levels. Not like this at all. This is all dug out for the health and safety of the tourists." Grandpa made that harrumphing noise again.

The gemstones were quite unimpressive. In fact, Josh had trouble telling a gemstone from an ordinary stone. Grandpa was quite right when he had said the trick was in knowing one when you saw one. Then they went to see one of the gem cutters, a man Grandpa knew from his time out fossicking. He was quite old, probably about Grandpa's age, and had apparently been cutting gems for many many years. Fossickers brought the stones they had found to him to evaluate and cut if they were worth it.

"Got a young miner with you," he said, looking at Josh. "Make sure he plays fair and he's not a ratter. Wouldn't want him to end up in the bottom of a mine shaft."

Grandpa laughed. "He's a good boy this one. He'd never be a ratter."

The gem cutter brought out a small velvet tray of gems he had already cut. They were stunning. The light sparkled off the stones and the range of colours was amazing – from gold and yellow right through to orange, pink and blue. Even Auntie Pam was impressed. She was even more impressed when he brought out some rings for her to look at.

"That one's like Grandma's – look, Grandpa," she exclaimed. "Same colour, only hers was bigger, wasn't it?"

"Close in colour, but ours was about twice that size," said Grandpa.

"That would have been worth a pretty penny," said the gem cutter.

"Yes, she was, worth every penny of it."

CHAPTER 11

The next day they moved on. Grandpa wanted to get to Richmond, a bit more than 800 kilometres away. It was far further than they had travelled the first day, and Auntie Pam was not happy.

"Look, woman," he said. "We can easily do this in one day if we get up early and get on our way. The roads are good, and there won't be much traffic. We can get there by dark, and then we can have two nights at Richmond to rest up. Just pack up and don't dilly-dally. We'll get going just after dawn."

So they did. Kat had her swag ready to go just after dawn and helped Josh with his tent. He was getting better at packing up but her help was appreciated, and it made the job so much easier. Not as easy as her swag was to pack up though.

It was a long, long day. Grandpa didn't have the radio on and there nothing much to see out the window except lots of long, straight stretches of road and flat uninteresting country. It did give him a chance to talk with Kat, though. He found out her mother had died when Kat was four, and she didn't really remember much about her. She lived with her Dad on a cattle station in South Australia, and had done lessons through something called School of the Air until she was old enough to go to boarding school. There had been other children living on the cattle station. They had a governess who looked after them all and helped them with school work. Then Kat had gone to Adelaide and later to Sydney to boarding school, returning to the cattle station and her father on school holidays.

"Weren't you lonely after your Mum died, and being away from your Dad so much?" asked Josh.

He thought about how he felt after his Mum and Dad split up, and couldn't imagine how hard it would be without a Mum.

"Not really. I don't really remember Mum, and Dad was always there for me. We did everything together. We still do. Some of the other kids at the boarding school come from cattle stations too, so we have things in common, and we all know the school term is only ten or so weeks and then we get to go home. Some teachers can make it seem a lot longer though." She smiled. "I prefer it on the cattle station – I don't think I could ever live in a city."

Kat went on to describe the things she did on the cattle station. She had a horse, but now a lot of the work was done on motorbikes, and she had one of those too. Josh was envious.

"I go out mustering with Dad a lot, and we sleep under the stars in our swags. He lets me drive the ute now I'm tall enough and can reach the pedals. We don't have TV, and I honestly don't miss it. I read a lot – I always have. We have the internet now at the homestead, and I can get my 'technology fix' if I need it, and keep up with friends on email and Facebook. Mobiles don't work out there."

How different that was to his life, mused Josh. No wonder she wasn't scared to sleep out in the open. That also explained why she got on with Grandpa so well – she was used to living with and working with men, and found their conversation and company easy.

Finally they neared Richmond after passing through Hughenden. Grandpa said he thought there was a great fossil museum in Hughenden, but it was late in the day and everything was shut. Reaching Richmond, just as it got dark, they turned into the camping ground and piled out of the vehicle to stretch their cramped legs.

Auntie Pam organised the dinner, Josh and Kat set up their sleeping arrangements while Grandpa unpacked the rest of the gear. Josh eyed Kat's swag enviously, imagining how good it must be to be able to sleep in the open under the stars.

"I think we deserve an early night," said Grandpa. He sounded tired. "We'll stay here a couple of nights, I think. We'll check out some fossils tomorrow and have a bit of a look around. Might even find a dinosaur."

Yeah, right, thought Josh.

CHAPTER 12

First stop after breakfast was Kronosaurus
Corner – a Visitor Information Centre and
Museum on the main street of Richmond. There
was a huge statue of a sea monster on the corner,
its open mouth displaying lots of razor-sharp teeth.
Auntie Pam arranged everybody near the massive
open mouth to get a photo. Inside the Centre, after
Grandpa paid their admission fee, they entered the
fossil display area. The rooms were huge, with lots
of glass cases and display areas containing shells
and bones, and illustrations of the creatures they
came from – mostly weird sea dwellers that lived
around 100 million years ago.

They wandered from room to room until they found a gallery separated from the rest of the area by swing doors. As they went through, it took a minute for Josh's eyes to adjust to the dimmer light. Then he focused on an amazing display in the middle of the room. It was huge – the skeleton of an enormous sea creature that had been found near Richmond. Almost every bone was there, laid out just as the creature had died. Apparently a local farmer, Ian Levers, had found it in 1989. A team of people organised by the Queensland Museum had carefully excavated and reconstructed the skeleton he was looking at. Josh was mesmerized, fascinated by every detail of the fins – or were they flippers?

"Look – look – a dinosaur!" shouted Emily excitedly.

"Not exactly," replied Grandpa. "It's a pliosaur – a sea creature that lived over 100 million years ago. She's been nicknamed 'Penny the Plesiosaur'. She was a marine creature, not a dinosaur. Dinosaurs lived on land, not in the sea."

That detail didn't seem to matter to Emily. "It's a dinosaur! It's a dinosaur!" she chanted. "I told you dinosaurs were real," she said pointedly to Josh.

"But you just said it was a pliosaur, so why is she called Penny the Plesiosaur?" asked Auntie Pam.

"I think pliosaur is the name they gave the 'family' of creatures that lived around that time and looked like that. Plesiosaur was a more specific type – a sub species," explained Grandpa.

"Well, they should explain that better," said Auntie Pam. "It's confusing, especially to small children."

Ever the teacher, thought Josh. Got to have everything exactly right. All this was irrelevant to Emily who was happily dancing around the outside of the display case, chanting "Dinosaur, dinosaur, dinosaur."

Kat joined in the conversation. "Penny the Plesiosaur was a giant marine animal that lived in the Eromanga Sea, a huge sea that covered almost half of Australia, from up where Darwin is now all the way down to South Australia. Our cattle station used to be part of that sea. It went across Australia almost as far as Mount Morgan, where we camped the first night, almost to the line of volcanoes that produced the gemstones Grandpa showed us at Rubyvale."

Grandpa nodded approvingly. "You know your ancient history, Kat."

Kat smiled. "I'm a bit of a book worm. I love reading about ancient history. I have a lot of time to read when I'm home on the cattle station."

Josh wondered why he hadn't known these things, why he hadn't studied ancient Australia in school. He was starting to appreciate there was a lot he didn't know.

"So, what happened to the Eromanga Sea?" he asked.

"It came and went, three times, I think," said Kat. "Between 110 million years ago and a 100 million years ago or thereabouts. The sea level rose and fell as parts of the sea formed and disappeared. And when it wasn't covered in water, the land was covered in massive areas of forest that eventually rotted down. That's what made coal and I think the gas deposits they're mining now." She looked to Grandpa for approval.

"Pretty much, Kat. Hard to believe when you look at the country now – dry and dusty. Certainly hard to believe there was rainforest growing."

Josh reflected on the countryside he had seen on the drive the previous day – grassy plains with a few trees, rocky and dry in places. Grandpa said there had been rain in the previous year and things were looking pretty good. He couldn't imagine what it looked like at other times if this was 'pretty good'. The grass was brown, not green as it was on the Gold Coast. It was spindly, but there were quite a lot of cattle grazing on the land.

"Dinosaurs, dinosaurs, dinosaurs," chanted Emily happily, oblivious to the conversation going on around her. "I knew there were dinosaurs," she chanted as they left the gallery and went to get something to eat at the café.

Later that afternoon, while Grandpa had a snooze and Auntie Pam and Emily went down to the lake by the camping ground, Josh and Kat explored the little town. There wasn't a lot to explore as Richmond was a small town, but the main street was interesting. The rubbish bins were pretty amazing, made to look like the open mouth of a pliosaur. Lots of signs told stories about what the town was like in the olden days. Josh was surprised how many buildings had burnt down over the years. It seemed that there wasn't a local fire brigade to put the fires out like there is in modern towns and cities. Kat was impressed by a beautiful statue of a stockman and his horse, both made from bits of scrap metal welded together. Josh took a photo for her on his phone and promised to email it to her when they got back. She was great company, and he was glad she had been able to come on the trip. And he did envy her swag – and was wondering how he could get one for himself.

CHAPTER 13

The plan for the next day was to drive to Winton, only a little more than 200 kilometres away. Apparently Grandpa and Grandma had used Winton as a base when they had been outback hunting for gemstones and opals. Auntie Pam was still insisting they stay in camping grounds or caravan parks. Grandpa was still grumbling – saying, "Grandma and I used to bush camp all the time. This camping ground business is just a waste of money."

Auntie Pam was insistent it wasn't safe to set up camp in the middle of nowhere with children, and if money was an issue, she'd pay. Josh wondered what she'd say if she knew Kat and her Dad bush camped all the time and actually preferred it.

As they loaded the camping gear into the ute, Josh found an opportunity to talk about Kat's swag. "This swag is really cool, Grandpa," he said, as he passed it up to him in the ute. "So much easier than a tent and quicker to set up. Kat uses hers all the time when she's out with her Dad."

Grandpa nodded. "Kat's a pretty lucky girl. She's got a Dad who doesn't mollycoddle her." He glanced over to Auntie Pam. "She's going to grow up to be a mighty fine young person. As are you," he added, looking at Josh. Josh felt a surge of pride. He wasn't sure what to say, so he said nothing.

Winton turned out to be bigger than Richmond, and they had a choice of camping grounds. Grandpa chose the one furthest from town. The first thing Josh noticed were the rubbish bins that were made to look like dinosaur feet. That was going to set Emily right off on dinosaurs again, he thought. He still wasn't convinced about the dinosaurs. Everything he'd heard and seen so far had been about marine fossils from a long ancient sea. Marine creatures weren't dinosaurs, he was certain of that. But he wasn't going to get into an argument. Better to keep the peace with Auntie Pam.

They set up camp and went into town to buy supplies. Grandpa knew his way around as he had been there many times before. While Auntie Pam and Emily went into the bakery for tea and cakes, he took Josh and Kat into the shop next door. It was a long, narrow shop that seemed to sell almost everything.

"This is Searle's," Grandpa said. "Been here as long as I can remember, probably as long as anyone in town can remember. If you need anything Searle's will have it, from boots and hats to sewing needles."

They wandered through the shop. Grandpa certainly was right. Clothes, hats, tablecloths, souvenirs, mugs, children's toys, plumbing supplies, camping gear – even swags. Josh stood in front of the swags stacked on the rack. There was quite an assortment. Kat came over and explained the different types.

"That's what I've got," she said pointing to one on the lower shelf. "Dad's got one of these," pointing to one on the middle shelf. "They're heavier – they're an older type. I think he's had his for a long time. They last for years and years."

Josh lifted one off the lower shelf. It was about the same weight as Kat's, but it smelled new – a sort of canvas smell that he quite liked. He looked at the price tag. It wasn't cheap, but then Kat said they last forever. Mum had given him some spending money, but not that much. He wondered if he could borrow some from Grandpa. There would be no point in asking Auntie Pam – she wouldn't approve.

Grandpa had been talking to an older man behind the counter. He had been asking about some people he knew in town, and about the road conditions. Apparently the man behind the counter knew all about what was going on in town.

"Lark Quarry is open," he told them. "Road's a bit rough but passable, and the free camping area at the waterhole's open. Need to take your own firewood though, but there's plenty around on the road out. Opalton is quiet at this time of the year."

"Wouldn't mind a day or two out there," responded Grandpa. "Actually, a week or two would be even better."

Over dinner that night Grandpa told them what he and Grandma used to do. They had a favourite place where they would look for opals at Opalton. They used to stay for a month or two in the camper, only going to Winton when they needed supplies.

"That's what we did on our trips away," said Grandpa. "We'd go to Rubyvale and camp at Reward, then to Opalton, then to Lightning Ridge and camp at Three Mile Flat. Sometimes we'd find something worthwhile, but mostly not. It wasn't about finding a fortune – we just enjoyed the adventure together." He looked sad. "I miss her."

Auntie Pam looked at him in the flickering firelight. "I'm sure you do, and I understand how much you miss her. We all do. You had some wonderful adventures together."

CHAPTER 14

Grandpa and Auntie Pam must have had a talk later that night, because the next morning it was announced they were driving to Opalton to 'bush camp' in an area where Grandpa and Grandma used to go. It would give Grandpa a chance to visit an old haunt. It was his trip as much as a trip for the rest of them, and it was something he really wanted to do. Before they left Winton, Grandpa took the ute into town to get some extra supplies. The rest of them played on the 'musical fence' – an area on the edge of town where someone had built a drum kit and some other musical instruments out of scraps of metal. The main attraction was a length of fence where the wires had been stretched tight and 'tuned' so they made different sounds when hit with a piece of plastic pipe. They had a lot of fun trying to make a tune together.

The road to Opalton was dirt, more dirt and dust, with lots of corrugations and dips and signs saying 'Flooding – indicators show depth'. It was so dry Josh couldn't imagine there ever being any water in the dips, let alone a flood. It was too noisy in the ute to hear what Grandpa was saying, so Josh resolved to ask him when they made camp.

At Opalton a series of even rougher tracks headed out in various directions. A few old humpies made out of corrugated iron, and caravans were scattered around the area. Somehow Grandpa picked up the track he wanted. They all looked the same to Josh. There were no signs apart from a few that said 'Private – Keep Out'. They pulled up in a cleared barren area that had obviously been used as a camp in the past.

"Home sweet home," smiled Grandpa. "Best campsite in the world. Lots of 'no's here – no power, no water, no neighbors, no noise, and no charge."

They got out and surveyed the scene. Desolate was a word that came to Josh's mind. Rocks, dirt, prickly little bushes, more dirt and stones. Whatever did Grandpa see in this place? The look on Auntie Pam's face seemed to echo his thoughts.

Kat scrambled out after him. "Got the tarp, Grandpa?" she asked. "We can rig up some shade over there by that tree." Grandpa pulled out the tarp and in no time at all he and Kat had tied it up to create a cool shady area.

"Shall I get out the table and chairs and put the tent up over there?" asked Josh.

"Table and chairs are a good idea, boy," responded Grandpa, "but don't worry about the tent. Use this instead if you like." He pointed to a rolled up canvas bag on the floor of the camper. It was a swag! The swag he had looked at in Searle's! Josh beamed from ear to ear.

"Saw you looking at it in Searle's and thought you might like to give it a try. We can always take it back if you don't like it."

"Like it! That's awesome, Grandpa! Thank you so much! Of course I want to use it!"

Kat chose a good place to roll out both swags. He watched her kick away the small rocks and smooth the gravel and dirt to make a flat surface before she unrolled her swag. He did the same, and unrolled his very own new swag, smelling the new canvas smell. His own swag!

Even Auntie Pam seemed to be getting the idea. She used a nearby bush to hang out the towels they had used in the shower the night before, and busied herself setting up a camp kitchen under the shade of the tarp.

"Now, the rules," said Grandpa. "Be careful where you walk – there are mine holes out here.

Always wear shoes, and don't put your hands into any spaces except your pockets because there are things that bite living in holes. And don't be a ratter. Oh, and go out in pairs – don't wander off alone. Always tell someone which direction you're going, and take a mate."

Josh remembered the word 'ratter', but couldn't remember what it meant, so he asked.

"A ratter is someone who steals something from someone else's claim, like a gemstone or an opal," explained Grandpa. "Ratters are thieves, and they can end up getting their legs accidentally broken or falling down mine shafts."

'Right," said Josh. "Now I remember."

They passed the afternoon exploring. Auntie Pam and Emily stayed close by the campsite while Grandpa, Kat and Josh walked around the surrounding area. Grandpa showed them holes in the ground, now covered with sheets of rusting iron or lumps of wood, where people had dug mines looking for opals. He explained how opals came in different shades and colours. Just because you found one, it didn't mean there were lots more in the same hole. There could be though, and that was what was so addictive. You just kept digging in the hope there was another one in the next shovel full of dirt. "Opalton is a place for people who live on hope and love a challenge," he said. "Most people only come here in the winter, but some crazies stay in the summer when it can get really hot. A few have died out here in the heat. I can show you some graves."

So different from the Gold Coast, thought Josh. Or was it really? He remembered what his mother had said about a few people on the Gold Coast – living on hopes and dreams.

That evening, with no lights showing from anywhere else, the glow from their firelight was brilliant and the stars shone brighter than ever. It was so quiet – it was a different world.

"Is it like this when you're out with your Dad on the cattle station?" Josh asked Kat.

"Almost," she replied. "Not as quiet as this, though. We have the noise of the cattle – and the horses, if we're using them. This is really quiet, like ghostly quiet." After a moment she added, "Ancient quiet."

"Yes, it is, isn't it, Kat," responded Grandpa. "This is a timeless place. It feels like it's been here for centuries – which it actually has. Millennia. The ancient seas, and then the forests, and now dry with the occasional floods."

"Is that why there are signs in some of the dips in the road – signs about flooding?" asked Josh.

"This is part of the Channel Country," explained Grandpa. "When it rains here the water pretty much covers everything and flows south through millions of channels – little dips and gullies that gradually join up to form creeks and rivers like Cooper Creek and the Diamantina River. The water eventually ends up in Lake Eyre way south in South Australia where Kat lives. It takes months for the water to reach there. Most of it doesn't – it soaks into the ground or is evaporated by the sun. But when it does rain heavily it can flood for miles, blocking the roads. Nobody goes anywhere for weeks."

Looking around, Josh could not imagine what it would look like – water flowing into gullies and creeks, covering the country like a great wet blanket. Later that night he snuggled into his new swag, staring up at the millions of stars. He mused on how old this land was and how it had changed over millions of years, from seas to forest to almost desert. He could hear Kat quietly breathing in the swag next to him – she must be asleep already. He was grateful she had put her swag next to his.

While he was delighted to be sleeping in the open, he was not yet ready to be away from the safety of others. He snuggled further down into his swag and closed his eyes. He could feel the ground underneath him, not as soft as the camp bed he had been sleeping on in the tent. Wriggling to get comfortable, he felt a stone under his left shoulder. He must have missed it when he swept the ground before putting his swag down. He reached out and under and found the culprit, a cylindrical stone tapered at one end. It looked unusual. A bluish light reflected off it in the moonlight. He held it up in the soft light, turning it, watching the colour change. He'd have a better look in the light of morning. Maybe it was an opal he thought, as he drifted off to sleep.

CHAPTER 15

Josh woke next morning to the sound of Grandpa working in their camp kitchen, boiling the billy to make his cup of tea. Kat was already up, sitting on a camp chair next to Grandpa. There was no sign of the others – they must still be asleep in the camper.

"Morning, young man," said Grandpa. "Sleep well in your swag?"

"It was great," Josh replied. "Under the stars is the very best place to sleep. I can see why Kat likes it so much. And the swag was really comfortable. Thanks heaps Grandpa."

"You're welcome Josh. Makes me feel good to be able to give you something you really want. Kids can be so difficult to buy presents for. I never know what newfangled thing you kids are using, and I used to leave it up to Grandma to sort it all out." He sighed. Then he changed the subject. "Anyway, Kat and I were just talking about what we should do today. I think we should drive out to Lark Quarry."

"Lark Quarry? Why would larks live out here?" asked Josh. "There's nothing much for birds to live on, and no water."

Grandpa laughed. "That's not why it's called Lark Quarry. It got its name from a man who did a lot of work there. Queensland Museum named it after him to recognise the work he did for them, in the heat and the flies, for no pay I might add."

"Why did Queensland Museum want work done out here?" asked Josh.

"Wait and see boy, just wait and see," responded Grandpa.

+++

After Auntie Pam and Emily got ready they all piled into the ute. Auntie Pam was concerned about leaving all the camping gear, once again worried it could get stolen. Grandpa said "Harrumph, don't be silly woman, nobody would steal from a campsite out here. That's ratting and nobody does that." Josh had his hand in the pocket of his jeans and felt the stone he had picked up in the night – the one he thought might be an opal. He had meant to show it to Grandpa, but they had been busy talking about other things. What if it was an opal? Would that mean he was a ratter? If it was a stone surely it wouldn't matter, but if it was an opal it might be worth a lot of money. And then he could pay Grandpa back for the swag and maybe get a decent present for his Mum for her next birthday. But then would he be a ratter? Was this somebody's opal claim? If so, someone might claim the opal and come to break his legs and throw him down a mine shaft ... Josh pushed the stone further down into his pocket, feeling guilty for having picked it up, but not guilty enough to put it back. He'd think about what to do later. They were coming back to this place to camp, so he could put it back tonight.

The road from Opalton to Lark Quarry was even worse than the one they had been on the previous day. Not that you could call it a road. It was a dusty, bumpy track with lots and lots of shallow gullies they had to cross. Josh even had to get out and open a gate at one place, so they could keep on the track. And then, around a small series of red hills covered in spindly bushes, they saw it. Lark Quarry, a low building that looked as if it was built into the side of a hill. Actually, it *was* built into the side of a hill. Grandpa hadn't said anything about that!

CHAPTER 16

Josh looked around in amazement while Grandpa and Auntie Pam paid for the entry tickets. There was a tour starting in ten minutes, so they were just in time. On the walls were enormous pictures of dinosaurs. Emily was ecstatic, dancing around and pointing. "Dinosaurs, dinosaurs, dinosaurs," she shrilled.

The tour began. They were led into a dark, cavernous room. The guide started talking.

"Ninety-five million years ago something happened here, a moment in time preserved forever in the rocks. I would like you all to imagine what this area looked like 95 million years ago. The great inland sea had receded and this land was covered in lush vegetation, with huge trees. Inland lakes and billabongs fed by streams provided ample water for a myriad of plants to grow. And feeding on those plants were dinosaurs of many shapes and sizes, from small bird-like dinosaurs right up to massive sauropods many times larger than an elephant. Most were vegetarians, but amongst them were some carnivores, feeding on the smaller dinosaurs. There was a waterhole here back then – we don't know how big, but this place was right on the edge of the water where dinosaurs came to drink. We know this, because preserved in the mud at the edge of this waterhole are footprints, footprints of hundreds of small dinosaurs."

The guide turned on her torch and shone it in the ground in front of the group. Her light illuminated the outlines of many three-toed footprints in the rock. She moved the light from footprint to footprint. Josh was mesmerised.

"The interesting thing is that most of these footprints are heading in the same direction," she continued. "That's odd, because you'd expect a group of animals at a waterhole to be milling about, turning this way and that. The other odd thing is that we believe these small dinosaurs were running. You can see the footprints are deeper at one end than the other, so their weight wasn't distributed evenly. They were putting more pressure on one part of their feet than another. They were running. But why were they running?"

She paused for dramatic effect.

"They were running from something, something they were scared of. They were in danger." Again she paused. "From this." And she shone her light on a much bigger footprint. This footprint also had three toes, but it was much bigger, at least five times bigger than the others.

"We believe this is a footprint of a theropod, a meat eating dinosaur. We believe he or she was chasing the other dinosaurs, trying to catch one to eat. He ran this way ..." She shone her light on another huge footprint, and then another. "He or she turned here – you can see this footprint is deeper on one side. The smaller dinosaurs scattered – see where they've run away." She extended her light to show a lot of smaller footprints heading in all directions. Then she turned the main lights on to reveal the entire scene, with thousands of footprints preserved in the rock in front of them.

They stood in silence and looked in amazement. People in the group moved along the edge of the boardwalk surrounding the footprints, taking photos and pointing at various places.

"This very spot is the site of a dinosaur stampede – the largest preserved record of a dinosaur stampede in the world. It's now a world heritage site, excavated and preserved, thanks to the work of many people, including paleontologists from the Queensland Museum. This area is named after Malcolm Lark, a man who did a great deal of work initially uncovering these dinosaur trackways. This site is on the Australian National Heritage list as the Dinosaur Stampede National Monument. That means it's been deemed to have outstanding significance to the nation, and is to be preserved and protected."

Josh was quiet as they filed out of the room. So, dinosaurs, real dinosaurs did exist right here in Queensland. He would have to concede that to Emily and Grandpa, but he still had a few questions. All they had were footprints, and that was a long way from knowing how big they really were and what they looked like. That was speculation. And as for dragons – that was definitely fiction.

CHAPTER 17

They returned to their campsite at Opalton, and that night, around the campfire, Grandpa told them more about opals and dinosaurs and the trips he and Grandma had made to this area.

"The first I heard about dinosaurs was when we were mining opals at Lightning Ridge," he said. "We would find the odd opalised shell, remnants from the great inland sea – the Eromanga Sea. They were pretty. Opal would form in the crevices and holes in the fossilised shells. Then we started to hear about opals being found in fossilised bone – bone fragments, particularly bones that had natural hollow areas in them. I saw some, and we would chip or grind away the bone to get at the opal. I heard about someone who found a fossilised jaw bone. The opal had formed in the holes where the teeth had been. They said it was a dinosaur jaw. That was the first time I'd heard about dinosaurs being out here."

He paused and then continued. "I believe they've found some bones and even teeth, but I haven't heard of them finding skulls or anything like that. It's sad that the opals are more precious than the fossils, so the bones are destroyed. It's good that Lark Quarry has been preserved, even if they haven't found any bones there."

"So, all we have are footprints – no real bones that prove what dinosaurs were like?" asked Josh.

"Oh no," interjected Kat. "They've found bones, lots of bones, all the way from where we were at Richmond right down to the south coast of Victoria and South Australia. I'm pretty sure if we tried hard we could find something on our property. It's just that the area is so big, no one has the time or the money to start looking. Lots of fossils have been found by accident – like at Lark Quarry. That was found by someone looking for opal who happened to recognise a dinosaur footprint when he saw it."

"But all we saw today were footprints. They're not fossils – they're just footprints," said Josh.

"The footprints are called trace fossils," Kat continued. "My teacher explained to me they're called that because they can show us traces of what the actual animals were like. They're not the actual animals but indications of animals, of course, but they *are* signs that animals had been there. Things like footprints, tooth marks, and even dinosaur poo are all trace fossils."

"Dinosaur poo," shrieked Emily "Yuck! Who'd want to be interested in dinosaur poo?"

"Lots of people," retorted Kat. "From that they can tell what dinosaurs ate and how they digested food, and then the scientists would have an idea of maybe how big their stomachs were, and then how big they were. The poo also shows what was growing here back then. Lots of really important information."

"So if they ever found a tooth, that might confirm what they ate as well?" asked Josh.

"Sure," continued Kat. "I imagine it would be pretty rare to find a tooth, but if they did find one, that would definitely help them determine what dinosaurs ate. It's like a massive mystery puzzle where the scientists try to tie all the clues together to get a better idea of what the dinosaurs were like."

They sat in silence for a moment, and then Kat added. "You remember those footprints we heard about at Mount Morgan? They are trace fossils. The dinosaurs didn't actually dance on the ceiling. Those footprints are called 'casts'. The dinosaur foot imprints would had been made in what was then mud. The imprint would have filled with clay or something that set harder than the mud. When the miners dug the cavern they found the underneath bits – the 'casts' are actually the imprints made from above. They were looking at them from underneath."

That night, tucked up in his swag under a million stars, Josh wondered about the prehistoric world. So, there were dinosaurs walking around at Mount Morgan and out here at Opalton. Was it possible he could be lying in the very spot a dinosaur had slept? Did dinosaurs sleep, and if they did, did they sleep standing up or lying down? And Kat had also mentioned she thought dinosaurs laid eggs – how could that be? He could be sleeping right now where a dinosaur nest had been. And teeth – imagine being able to tell what a dinosaur ate from looking at a tooth. As he drifted off to sleep his hand touched the stone he had found the previous night. It was shaped a bit like a tooth. What if it wasn't an opal, but a dinosaur tooth instead? If he kept it, would he be a ratter, or would he have something that was so precious and ancient he should give it to the Queensland Museum? Maybe they would put it on display with his name on it and he would be famous like Malcolm Lark ...

CHAPTER 18

Josh was sad they had to leave Opalton. They had to drive back to Winton to get food, and time was running out. Soon they would need to start the long trip back to the Gold Coast. He rolled up his swag and put it in the ute next to Kat's.

Auntie Pam insisted they stay in the camping ground in Winton. She said they all needed showers and she wanted to do some washing. Grandpa said he had one more surprise for them. He also had some more people he wanted to catch up with.

The next morning they headed out of Winton. About ten kilometres out of town Grandpa took a side road past a sign that had a huge dinosaur carved on it, and a notice underneath saying 'Australian Age of Dinosaurs'. "I've never been here," he told them, "but they told me in town it's worth coming to see."

As they approached the reception building they saw a life-like statue of a dinosaur that looked a lot like the picture of one they had seen at Lark Quarry, the one that had chased the smaller dinosaurs. Its open mouth had rows of sharp, cruel teeth. Josh fingered the stone in his pocket. He still hadn't told Grandpa he had it, or shown anyone else, not even Kat. He felt a bit guilty about taking it from Opalton.

A guide in a uniform was coming out of the building as they walked to the entrance. "Hi there," she said. "Welcome to the Age of Dinosaurs. This is Banjo – he was a theropod. I don't know if you've been to Lark Quarry, but if you have you may recognise his footprints."

They assured her they had, and they definitely recognised Banjo's footprints. Emily said she was glad he hadn't been there when she was there. She didn't want to be his lunch or dinner. The guide laughed.

"Don't worry – we've already fed Banjo today," she joked. "So it's safe to pat him and even put your head in his mouth if you like." So Josh put his head right into Banjo's gaping mouth and she took a group photo of them all. That would be something to show the kids back at school.

The first part of the Age of Dinosaurs tour was a talk in the collection room. Like Lark Quarry, the room was dark, and when they went in Josh could barely make out the displays. The tour guide explained how dinosaur bones had been found by accident by graziers out on their properties when they were mustering stock. Dinosaur digs were then organised, and when bones were dug up they were carefully brought back to special areas called 'prep' areas. There the bones were carefully separated from the surrounding rock, and then paleontologists could identify and piece together the bones to make up as much of the skeleton as they could. Some bones were large and pretty much intact, but others were shattered into many small fragments.

The spotlight lit up a skeleton of Banjo, the replica dinosaur they had seen outside, the one that did the chasing at Lark Quarry. The tour guide explained how, from the length of the leg bones and the size of the claws and the teeth, they could determine the size of the animal and the way it moved.

"Teeth," though Josh. "They've found teeth!" He fingered the stone in his pocket.

The spotlight then fell on a display of the actual bones of Banjo. Real 95 million year-old bones. Bones of an animal that had lived right here in Australia. There was no disputing it now, thought

Josh. Emily was right. Dinosaurs did exist, and they lived right here in Australia.

The spotlight then moved to another display of bones, those of a much bigger dinosaur – a sauropod. It had been around sixteen metres long and two and a half metres high. This was apparently quite a small sauropod – bones from even bigger ones had been found. The guide explained that this animal would have been a vegetarian, and one of the ways to tell was by looking at their teeth. Josh fingered that stone in his pocket again.

They walked over to the preparation lab for the second part of their tour. This was the building the bones were brought to after they were dug up, and trained 'preppers' carefully chipped or ground away the surrounding rock from around the bone. They gathered with a group of others waiting for the tour to start. It didn't look much like a lab to

Josh. Nothing like the clean white organised space he imagined when he thought of a lab. This place was big and dusty, and there was a lot of noise and people milling about. Nobody had white coats.

The tour guide turned on his microphone and started to explain how local farmer, David Elliot, had started the Age of Dinosaur Museum after he found a bone sticking out of the ground on his property near Winton. Since then lots more bones had been found, and they were discovering more all the time. In fact, they already had enough bones to keep the lab going for fifty years.

They walked past a huge floor-to-ceiling racking system, stacked full of what looked like huge white rocks with labels written on them. The guide explained they contained bones that had been dug up, wrapped carefully in plaster of paris to protect them, as a broken leg would be, and then brought to the lab to be worked on. At the far end of the room bones lay on the floor. They were allowed to touch these massive bones.

The guide said, "Take the opportunity now, because who knows when you'll get another chance to touch a 95 million year-old dinosaur."

Josh ran his fingers over the bones, as did Grandpa, Kat, and Emily who was quite subdued. Even she was in awe at the size of the bones.

In another area of the prep lab a group of people were working on the real dinosaur bones, painstakingly grinding the rock away with what looked like little dental drills. As the guide explained, this was the first time these bones had been exposed for 95 million years, and what an honour and a privilege it was to be the first person to see and touch a bone like that. They were allowed to talk to the people working on the bones, and to ask questions if they wished.

Five or six people were working on large bones – ribs and leg bones from what they were told by the guide were sauropod bones. But they wouldn't be absolutely sure it was a sauropod until the paleontologist had assessed the finished bones.

Further along, two people were working on smaller bones. Josh stopped in front of one person who was working on a very small piece of bone, looking at it through a magnifying glass. When he saw Josh was interested in what he was doing, he stopped and turned the magnifying glass around to show Josh what he was working on.

"We think it's a bit of Banjo's jaw," he said. "There are a lot of small pieces here and we're hoping to find enough pieces to be able to reconstruct at least part of his jaw. See here," he said, pointing to a hole in the bone. "We think this is a tooth cavity."

"Have you found any teeth?" asked Josh.

"Yes we have," he replied. "A few, but we'd really like to find more." Josh felt the shape of the stone in his pocket. It was too much – he couldn't resist, so he pulled it out and showed the man.

"Do you think this could be a tooth? I found it out near Opalton. I didn't really steal it or anything – I just found it on the ground, and I was wondering ..." He tailed off, not sure what else to say or if he had already said too much and would get into trouble. The man put the stone under the microscope and carefully rotated it under the light.

"George," he called out. "Come and have a look at this." Another man came over, obviously someone important, as he had a uniform on. George sat down and carefully took Josh's little stone and held it under the light, turning it over, examining all sides. Then he picked up the little drill the other man had been using and started to drill along one side. He carefully blew away the dust with a little air jet.

"Where did you get this?" he asked Josh.

"Out near Opalton," he blurted out. "I was with my Grandpa and I found it on the ground. Honest, I didn't dig it up or anything, I'm not a ratter. It was underneath my swag and I just found it. I don't want to get into any trouble."

By then Grandpa had come over to see what was going on, and Kat and Auntie Pam and Emily joined them. Now he was in trouble – he should have told Grandpa when he first found it.

George looked up at the gathered group. "Well, young man, you may have found something very significant. I can't be sure until we do a lot more work, but this could well be a dinosaur tooth. And from what you tell me about where you found it, it's from the right area. There are often fossils found in opal areas – they're of a similar geological age. Are you with this lad?" he asked Grandpa.

"Sure am," said Grandpa. "We were bush camping the other night just south of Opalton, not far from Lark Quarry."

"Well," continued George, "I'd like to keep this, if you're happy to donate it, of course." Looking at Josh, he continued, "As I said, I can't guarantee it, but this little fossil is definitely worth investigating further. The colour and texture are indicative of fossilised tooth material. It'll be up to the experts to decide, but I've been working on fossils for a while and I can tell you it looks very promising."

Josh was almost lost for words. "Yeah, sure, I mean of course, wow, imagine – a dinosaur tooth!"

"Josh found a dinosaur tooth?" chimed in Emily. "From a real dinosaur? What kind of dinosaur? A new kind of dinosaur?"

"Possibly," replied George. "We're finding new types of dinosaurs all the time. Just recently they found some feathered dinosaur fossils in China. Imagine – feathered dinosaurs. They could possibly be the precursor of birds, part of the evolutionary chain. They've given this new dinosaur a scientific name, *Beibeilong sinensis*, which when translated into plain English means 'Chinese baby dragon'."

"See, see, SEE!" shouted Emily gleefully. "I told you! I knew I was right! Dinosaurs and dragons DID EXIST!"

Josh looked over at Grandpa and winked. "I guess we should go and see if we can find a unicorn now, Grandpa?"